OLD HOUSE, NEW HOUSE

by
Phillis Gershator

illustrated by
Katherine Potter

Marshall Cavendish Children

All rights reserved
Marshall Cavendish Corporation
99 White Plains Road, Tarrytown, NY 10591
www.marshallcavendish.us/kids

Library of Congress Cataloging-in-Publication Data
Gershator, Phillis.
Old house, new house / by Phillis Gershator ; illustrated by
Katherine Potter. — 1st ed.
p. cm.
Summary: A child spends a wonderful summer in the country,
in a big old house with plenty of mice but no running water,
and begs to stay there, but summer's end and a cross-country
journey bring a wonderful surprise.
ISBN 978-0-7614-5386-4
[1. Dwellings—Fiction. 2. Country life—Fiction. 3. Summer—
Fiction. 4. Stories in rhyme.] I. Potter, Katherine, ill. II. Title.

PZ8.3.G3235Old 2008
[E]—dc22

2007022135

The illustrations are rendered in chalk pastels.
Book design by Vera Soki
Editor: Margery Cuyler

Printed in Malaysia
First edition
1 3 5 6 4 2

mc Marshall Cavendish
Children

With thanks to David, Diane, and Margery
—P.G.

For my daughters,
who never cease to amaze me
—K.P.

We moved to a big house—
there was a little house, too—
out in the country where
the fruit trees grew.

The house had no pipes,
no faucets, no sink,
but it had a well
and good water to drink.

and a cranberry bog
and a bullfrog creek
and mice in the wall—
I could hear them squeak.

I made friends with the mice
and the family down the road
and the pigs that oinked
and the rooster that crowed.

I made friends with the cat
who curled 'round my legs.
I made friends with the hens
when they laid their eggs.

I picked wild berries
and baked fruit pies
and hung sticky paper
to catch all the flies.

I bathed in a washtub
and soaped right up
and brushed my teeth
with water from a cup.

It was the very best summer I ever had,
then summer was over,
and I felt so sad.

"No, no," I said,
"I don't want to go.
I like it here.
I want to see snow!"

"I'll miss my new friends!
Who'll feed the mice?
I thought we'd build snowmen
and skate on the ice."

"Once it snows,"
said the grown-ups,
"we'll be all alone
in this old, old house
with no heat and no phone."

And so we left
and said farewell
to the cranberry bog
and the cold-water well.

How I hated to see
that summer end
and the house I loved
disappear 'round the bend.

I cried a lot
'cause I didn't know then
if I'd ever see snow
or make a new friend.

We drove and drove
through city and town . . .

. . . 'cross fields and deserts,
up mountains and down.

We drove out west
and what did we see?
A new house for us . . .

and new friends for me!